For more than forty years,
Yearling has been the leading name
in classic and award-winning literature
for young readers.

Yearling books feature children's
favorite authors and characters,
providing dynamic stories of adventure,
humor, history, mystery, and fantasy.

Trust Yearling paperbacks to entertain,
inspire, and promote the love of reading
in all children.

OTHER YEARLING BOOKS YOU WILL ENJOY

MOXY MAXWELL DOES NOT LOVE *STUART LITTLE*, *Peggy Gifford*

MOXY MAXWELL DOES NOT LOVE WRITING
THANK-YOU NOTES, *Peggy Gifford*

HARRIET THE SPY®, *Louise Fitzhugh*

DOGS DON'T TELL JOKES, *Louis Sachar*

BALLET SHOES, *Noel Streatfeild*

100 CUPBOARDS, *N. D. Wilson*

ALVIN HO: ALLERGIC TO GIRLS, SCHOOL, AND
OTHER SCARY THINGS, *Lenore Look*

Moxy Maxwell Does Not Love Practicing the Piano

(but she does love being in recitals)

By Peggy Gifford

Photographs by Valorie Fisher

A YEARLING BOOK

Text copyright © 2009 by Peggy Gifford
Photographs copyright © 2009 by Valorie Fisher

All rights reserved. Published in the United States by Yearling, an imprint of Random House Children's Books, a division of Random House, Inc., New York. Originally published in hardcover in the United States by Schwartz & Wade Books, an imprint of Random House Children's Books, a division of Random House, Inc., New York, in 2009.

Yearling and the jumping horse design are registered trademarks of Random House, Inc.

Grateful acknowledgment is made to The Creative Company for permission to reprint an excerpt from "The Elephant Bird" from *Swan Song* by J. Patrick Lewis, copyright © 2003 by J. Patrick Lewis. Reprinted by permission of The Creative Company.

Photograph of Miss America courtesy of the Ohio Historical Society.

Visit us on the Web! www.randomhouse.com/kids

Educators and librarians, for a variety of teaching tools, visit us at www.randomhouse.com/teachers

The Library of Congress has cataloged the hardcover edition of this work as follows:
Gifford, Peggy Elizabeth.
Moxy Maxwell does not love practicing the piano / by Peggy Gifford ; photographs by Valorie Fisher.
p. cm.
Summary: On the day of her recital, ten-year-old Moxy prepares for it in her usual flamboyant way which creates chaos at home.
ISBN 978-0-375-84488-1 (hardcover) — ISBN 978-0-375-96688-0 (glb) — ISBN 978-0-375-89289-9 (e-book)
[1. Concerts—Fiction. 2. Piano—Fiction. 3. Twins—Fiction. 4. Brothers and sisters—Fiction. 5. Humorous stories.]
I. Fisher, Valorie, ill. II. Title.
PZ7.G3635Ml 2009
[Fic]—dc22
2008036639

ISBN 978-0-375-85948-9 (pbk.)

Printed in the United States of America

10 9 8 7 6 5 4 3 2 1

First Yearling Edition

Random House Children's Books supports the First Amendment and celebrates the right to read.

In memory of my father
—P.G.

For Sam and Molly
—V.F.

Acknowledgments

I am grateful to Markie Ruzzo for her insight,
Donna Fitzpatrick for her support, and Anne
Schwartz for her invincible instincts.

—P.G.

I would like to thank my remarkably talented cast
of characters: Elinor, Charlie, Olive, Anne, and
David. I would like to thank Lee for her steady
hand behind the wheel, Tad for his extraordinary
patience, Aidan for all matters explosive, the town
of Cornwall for its spectacular stage, Emily for her
perfect yellow buttercup dress, Willa for her
fabulous pink gobs-of-glitter dress, and Peggy for
the wonderful, witty world of Moxy.

—V.F.

chapter 1
The Setup

It was just after 10:00 a.m. on Saturday, April 7, and Moxy Maxwell was still in bed. Outside, the temperature was sixty-four degrees. Inside, a slight (5 mph) breeze was coming through her open windows. Her white curtains were ballooning up and down as the wind came and went. Four or five birds were making chirping sounds. They were not exactly the chirping sounds Moxy was always reading about in books, but they were bird sounds just the same, reminding Moxy that she had almost forgotten about the fact of birds.

It was the perfect day not to wear a hat. The perfect day to put on her new red Windbreaker with the white piping and the three felt-lined pockets and go outside and see what was up. But Moxy didn't have time.

Moxy didn't have time because Moxy had a list of Nine Things to Do Before Tonight.

chapter 2
In Which We Learn About Tonight

Tonight Moxy Maxwell was going to make her Piano Debut at the Palace Theater. She and her sister, Pansy, who had just turned five (and still could not tie her shoes), were going to play a duet called "Heart and Soul."

chapter 3
Moxy Plays the Palace

The Palace Theater was only the biggest theater in town. It had 2,400 seats and was the place where all the Big Broadway Musicals played when they came on their national tours. Moxy's Piano Debut was being held at the unfashionable hour of 5 p.m. instead of the more civilized 7 p.m. because a very famous Rock Star (who no one but her mother had heard of) was scheduled to play the Palace at 8 p.m.

In fact, if Moxy's friend Sam hadn't

happened to have a mother who owned the Palace Theater in the first place, Moxy's Piano Debut wouldn't have been there at all. It would have been in the basement of Temple Emanuel on Lee Road.

chapter 4
In Which We Learn Two Things That Disappointed Moxy About Tonight

Two things disappointed Moxy about the recital tonight. The first was the fact that "Heart and Soul" was such a short song. She thought it should go on at least five minutes longer.

The second thing was that her twin brother, Mark Maxwell, who was seven minutes younger, was going to play a solo called "The Flight of the Bumblebee." Moxy thought that if Mark was going to play a solo then she, Moxy Maxwell, should be able to play a solo too.

But as Moxy thought about it, it didn't matter all that much because "The Flight of the Bumblebee" wasn't nearly as catchy as "Heart and Soul." In fact, it sounded like a bunch of bumblebees were swarming around your head. Sometimes Moxy would even find herself swatting in the direction of Mark when he was practicing it.

chapter 5
Moxy Maxwell's List of Nine Things She Had to Do Before Her Recital Tonight

Here is Moxy's List of Nine Things to Do Before Tonight:

1. Get out of bed.

2. Make sure her mother was back from Africa in time to bake the 150 cupcakes for the after-recital party Moxy was throwing.

3. Drink her Green Grass Power Shake so that she would have the upper-body strength to get through her recital.

4. Try on the capes that Granny George was making for Moxy and Pansy to wear.

5. Practice walking in the slippery silver tap shoes she was going to wear with the

cape. (She didn't want to slide all over the place when she made her Big Entrance.)

6. Try on her crown to make sure it wouldn't fall off when she made her Big Entrance.

7. Put on her stage makeup.

8. Warm up her voice in case someone asked her to sing.

9. Have the Big Dress Rehearsal.

Nine Things to Do Before Tonight
1. Get out of bed.
2. Make sure Mother is back from Africa.
3. Drink Green Grass Power milk shake
4. Try on the cape Granny George is making for tonight.
5. Practice walking around in the slippers/shoes
6. Walk around with crown on (could slide off!)
7. Put on stage make up.
8. Warm up voice in case someone asks me to sing tonight.
9. Have the Big Dress Rehearsal.

chapter 6
In Which Sam Calls

If I have not mentioned it before, I should now: Moxy Maxwell was very quick on the draw when it came to picking up her cell phone. In fact, her cell phone hadn't even finished the first note of Beethoven's Fifth when she answered it.

It was Sam.

"Are you nervous?" he said.

Even though Sam was a boy, and only six, he was Moxy's best friend. That was because Sam would do anything Moxy asked—and also, of course, because he was very nice.

"Nervous about what?" said Moxy. She was out of bed now and rummaging around in the bottom of her closet. She was looking for her silver tap shoes.

"Your piano recital," said Sam.

Even Sam knew it was a silly question. Moxy Maxwell had only been nervous once in her entire life and that was last August 23rd and it had only lasted for a paragraph. (See Chapter 25 of *Moxy Maxwell Does Not Love* Stuart Little.) In fact, Moxy was the opposite of nervous—Moxy could hardly wait for, as she called it, her Piano Debut.

"Can I come over and watch the Big Dress Rehearsal?" asked Sam.

Moxy, who was now looking under her bed for her left silver tap shoe, said, "Hurry up! I need all the help I can get."

Then Moxy and Sam hung up at exactly the same moment.

chapter 7
The Hook

The Hook is the part of a story that makes you, the Reader, want to keep reading to find out what happens next. Ideally, the Hook should come as early as Chapter 1— Chapter 2 at the latest. Any later, and the author risks "losing the reader." Which means that you, the Reader, might put this book down for just one second to get some gum and never come back. So please hang on—even though it is already Chapter 7, Something Really Big is about to happen.

chapter 8
Something Really Big

Downstairs, the Maxwells' phone rang. And Mrs. Maxwell, who was in the kitchen baking 150 cupcakes, wiped marshmallow frosting on her apron.

She picked up the phone on the third ring.

"Mrs. Maxwell?" It was Ms. Killingher. Ms. Killingher was Moxy and Mark and Pansy's piano teacher.

"Why, Ms. Killingher," said Mrs. Maxwell, "is anything wrong?" Moxy's mother knew that this had to be a busy day for

Ms. Killingher. Ms. Killingher was in charge of the whole recital, including all the announcements *and* the lights *and* the video camera *and* the programs *and* the tickets *and* the people who were supposed to take the tickets *and* the mother who was supposed to make the video.

"I'm about to print the programs for the recital tonight," said Ms. Killingher. "But before I do, I need to know how Moxy's practicing has gone this week."

"Moxy's practicing?" said Mrs. Maxwell absently. She was trying to remove some marshmallow frosting that had gotten mashed in her hair. "I'm sure it's gone very well," she went on, though she wasn't sure.

"So you feel confident Moxy will be able to *stop* playing her part of 'Heart and Soul' when she gets to the end?"

"*Stop* playing her part of 'Heart and Soul'?" said Mrs. Maxwell.

"And about the pounding," continued Ms. Killingher. "Has Moxy managed to stop that too?"

"Pounding?" said Mrs. Maxwell.

We have to forgive Mrs. Maxwell. She was feeling *very tired* this morning. You see, she'd just arrived home in the middle of the night from Africa.

chapter 9
In Which We Learn Why Mrs. Maxwell Was in Africa

Mrs. Maxwell had flown to Kenya, which is a country in Africa, last week at the last minute because her twin sister, Susan Standish, had fallen off a tippy ladder while she was feeding a giraffe. She had suffered a concussion. (The exact details of how it happened were still unclear, as was Aunt Susan Standish herself.)

Moxy had wanted to go with her mother. She wanted to talk to the president over there about getting a new flag. Number 39 on Moxy's list of all Possible Career Paths was to design flags for new countries and old countries that wanted to freshen up their look.

chapter 10

Which Begins with Ms. Killingher Saying, "Are You There, Mrs. Maxwell?"

"Are you there, Mrs. Maxwell?" said Ms. Killingher. Ms. Killingher thought Moxy's mother was behaving the *slightest bit* like Moxy today: She didn't seem to be listening.

There was a pause while Mrs. Maxwell realized how restful her trip to Kenya had been. Even though she had spent most of it sitting in an orange plastic chair at Nairobi General Hospital, reading a 1972 issue of *National Geographic*, while waiting for her sister to get unconfused enough to fly back home to Ohio.

"Mrs. Maxwell, did you get the note I sent home with Moxy last week?" continued Ms. Killingher.

"*Note?*" said Mrs. Maxwell. "I'm sure we did."

Mrs. Maxwell started to drag the phone across the kitchen floor to her husband's office, which was just ten feet away. But the cord attached to the wall got tangled in some marshmallow-frosted cupcakes just as she reached the hall outside his door.

"*I'm sure we got the note,*" Mrs. Maxwell said in a loud voice. Now she was staring at her husband, whose name was Ajax. (In addition to being Mrs. Maxwell's husband, Ajax was also Mark and Moxy's stepfather and Pansy's *real* father.)

But Ajax, who was also a famous children's poet, was too busy to think about *the note.* He was desperately trying to finish a poem he was writing about an extinct species called the elephant bird. The poem had been due yesterday.

The first verse was perfect. Here it is:

Eggs the size of dinosaur's
Legs as big as a beam
The Elephant Bird, the Elephant Bird
Was the ten-foot bird supreme.

Unfortunately, while Mrs. Maxwell had been in Africa, "The Elephant Bird" had slowed down considerably. That was because Ajax had been left in charge of *everything*. *Everything* might not seem like a lot. . . . But *everything* had stopped Ajax from finishing the second verse. All he needed was one more word.

Here is the second verse (minus the last word) so you can get an idea of what he was up against:

Claws as sharp as razor blades
Beak like a broad-head spear
The Elephant Bird, the Elephant Bird
Had nobody else to ___?___ .

Suggestions are welcome.

In fact, Ajax was so busy muttering to himself, "*Beak like a broad-head spear—the Elephant Bird—the Elephant Bird—had nobody else to . . . to what? To beer? To rear? To be near?*" that Mrs. Maxwell finally put the phone receiver down on the hall floor. Then she walked to the bottom of the stairs and called out, "Moxy?"

chapter 11
Encore

When Moxy didn't answer, Mrs. Maxwell called out again, "Moxy Anne?"

chapter 12
Once More!

When Moxy *still* didn't answer, Mrs. Maxwell called out one last time, "Moxy Anne Maxwell!"

chapter 13
In Which We Learn Why Moxy Anne Maxwell Did Not Reply

Moxy Anne Maxwell heard her mother calling. But she didn't answer. She didn't answer because she was in the guest room watching Aunt Susan Standish sleep. And Moxy didn't want to wake her. All the shades were drawn. It was quite dark. But you could still see Aunt Susan Standish's sleeping mask.

Aunt Susan Standish always slept in a sleeping mask. This one was made of white satin. It had quite a shine, as you can barely see from this photograph Mark took of it.

Mark is the most famous photographer in the neighborhood.

(Mark did not use a flash because he did not want to wake her.) Mark called this photograph "Sleeping Beauty."

"Sleeping Beauty," by Mark Maxwell.

Aunt Susan Standish was the most enchanting person Moxy had ever met. Sometimes Moxy couldn't believe that she was

Moxy's 100% Aunt and not just a Step-Aunt or a Half Aunt or a Family Friend Aunt. It meant that she and Aunt Susan Standish had some of the same genes. And Aunt Susan Standish's genes made Aunt Susan Standish do some very brave things.

One time Aunt Susan Standish was alone in a cage with an only somewhat tamed tiger. Another time she paddled down the Amazon in a tippy canoe, though she hadn't meant to. And sometimes she ate a flower instead of a salad for supper.

People always said that Moxy must have inherited her fearlessness from Aunt Susan Standish.

chapter 14
In Which There Is
a Diagnosis

"Is this how a coma looks?" whispered Pansy. Pansy was leaning over Aunt Susan Standish's face.

"No," whispered Moxy, "this is how unconscious looks."

"It is not, Moxy," said Mark. "She's just asleep."

"Is she awake?" Granny George shouted from the door.

"Not yet," said Aunt Susan Standish without so much as removing her mask or moving any body parts. "She'll be awake in twenty minutes."

Then it was silent . . . .
. . . . for
that long. Then Pansy said, "Aunt Susan
Standish can talk in a coma." Then everyone
got so busy telling everyone else to be quiet
that no one noticed Mrs. Maxwell standing
in the doorway.

chapter 15
Mrs. Maxwell Standing in the Doorway

Moxy hadn't seen her mother since she got back from Africa. And all week Moxy had worried that her mother might accidentally run into a lion. Or that a herd of buffalo might accidentally run into her. Moxy's mother wasn't fearless like Moxy and Aunt Susan Standish.

Moxy could hardly wait to show her mother the Surprise Outfits she and Granny George had been working on all week to wear to the recital tonight. But when Moxy saw her mother standing in the doorway wearing a sweatshirt with a big orange sun that said SMILE, YOU'RE IN MIAMI on it, she was a little startled by how tired her mother looked.

Here is a photograph Mark Maxwell took of Mrs. Maxwell's sweatshirt. It said SMILE, YOU'RE IN MIAMI.

"Mom, are you okay?" whispered Moxy. Actually, her whisper was so loud, it was a borderline "regular voice."

But Mrs. Maxwell was not okay. She was worried about her sister. She wanted to make sure no one woke her. So she did something only an experienced mother can do. She got everyone out of the room without saying a word. This is how she did it: She mouthed the word "OUT" while slicing her arms back and forth the way an umpire might.

It was very effective. Except for Mrs. Maxwell and Aunt Susan Standish, the room was evacuated in fewer than eighteen seconds.

As soon as Moxy and Pansy and Mark were gone, Mrs. Maxwell forgot all about finding out whether Moxy could stop playing her part of "Heart and Soul" tonight.

She also forgot about the note from Ms. Killingher. She also forgot about Ms. Killingher waiting on the phone.

Mrs. Maxwell went over to the bed to check on her sleeping sister.

chapter 16
Everything You Need to Know About the Green Grass Power Shake

Meanwhile, Moxy wandered downstairs. It was her plan to make a quite large glass of the Green Grass Power Shake. You may recall that drinking the Green Grass Power Shake was number three on Moxy's List of Nine Things to Do Before Tonight. The Green Grass Power Shake would give her the upper-body strength she needed to play "Heart and Soul."

The Green Grass Power Shake was very powerful: It had 1,433 combined vitamins and minerals—approximately 1,405 more than the *average* power shake. There was very little it couldn't do.

chapter 17
In Which Moxy
Is Helpful

The first thing Moxy noticed when she got downstairs was the phone cord. It was stretched like a clothesline across the kitchen floor and into the hall. Then she noticed that the phone was off the hook. So she hung it up.

The next thing Moxy did was step over the phone and into a big glob of marshmallow frosting. At first she thought it was gum. But as she walked on, she realized it had a *generally* sticky texture and not a *specifically* sticky texture, like normal gum.

It wasn't until she saw the 150 cupcakes

cooling on all the counters that she realized she was walking on marshmallow frosting.

Here is a photograph that Mark, who was already in the kitchen, took of the 150 cupcakes squished together on the counter-top. He called it "150 Cupcakes Made by 1 Mother in 183 Minutes."

"150 Cupcakes Made by 1 Mother in 183 Minutes," by Mark Maxwell.

chapter 18
In Which Something Smashes to the Floor and Breaks into Smithereens

Moxy went directly to the cupboard to get the jar of Green Grass Power Shake powder.

But it wasn't there. It wasn't on the first shelf, where it belonged. It wasn't on the second shelf, where it didn't belong. It was on the highest shelf, where it had never been before.

"Mark, could you please get the Green Grass Power Shake powder down?" asked Moxy.

But Mark just stood there taking

pictures of cupcakes, which is why it wasn't Moxy's fault she had to climb up on the counter. And reach a little higher than her comfort zone. And grab the jar of Green Grass Power Shake powder.

Just as it wasn't her fault when the Green Grass Power Shake powder slipped a little from her grip, bounced briefly on the counter, and exploded on the kitchen floor (taking down seven marshmallow-frosted cupcakes with it).

chapter 19

In Which the Question "How Green Was the Green Grass Power Shake Powder?" Is Answered

The Green Grass Power Shake powder was

> *a great and gorgeous green*
> *a lean*
> *mean*
> *light bright*
> *just right*
> *traffic light*
> *shade of green.*

And the Green Grass Power Shake powder was, well, it was everywhere. It was on the floor and on the counter and sifting through the air. And when the air cleared, Moxy could see that the Green Grass Power Shake powder was all over her mother's hair.

Here is a picture Mark miraculously took of the Green Grass Power Shake explosion just as it went off.*

*I think Mark used a Canon ZX with 1,873-mph-speed film and an aperture opening of just under 1 million to catch the Green Grass Power Shake powder in midair.

"Why, Mother!" said Moxy after the green dust had cleared. "I didn't hear you come in."

chapter 20
What Mrs. Maxwell Said to Moxy Next— a Short Quiz for the Reader

Q: What did Mrs. Maxwell say to Moxy next?

(Circle one)

1. "Oh, Moxy, sweetheart, are you hurt?"

2. "Don't worry, I had to wash my hair anyway—after all, today is *your* big day!"

3. "Darling, let me clean up this un-avoidable mess while you go upstairs and warm up your voice in case they ask you to sing tonight."

4. None of the above.

chapter 21
In Which We Learn the Correct Answer to the Quiz

And the correct answer is: 4!

chapter 22

In Which We Pause for a Chapter to Give Those of You Who Guessed the Right Answer an Opportunity to (Briefly) Congratulate Yourselves

chapter 23
What Mrs. Maxwell Really Said Next
OR
The Amazing Mind of a Tired Mother Who Is Not Too Tired to Focus

Even though there was Green Grass Power Shake powder in her hair and on her sweatshirt and all over her bunny slippers (with the happy exception of one left ear), Mrs. Maxwell said nothing about it. Instead, Mrs. Maxwell said, *"Where's the note from Ms. Killingher, Moxy?"*

chapter 24
About the Hum
in the House

Have you ever noticed how sometimes houses have hums running through them? You can't really hear a Hum in a House. But you know it's there—sort of the way you know that your own heart is beating—even if you're not exactly listening. It happens when everyone in the house is happy.

And just before Moxy spilled the Green Grass Power Shake powder all over her mother, everyone in the Maxwell house was happy.

Pansy was in Moxy's room trying on

one of the glitter crowns that Moxy had made for them to wear at their piano recital tonight. She was humming "Heart and Soul."

Granny George was happy. She was at her sewing machine out on the porch, enjoying the slight (5 mph) spring breeze coming from the northeast. She had almost finished stitching the red satin linings into the black velvet capes she was making for Moxy and Pansy to wear.

And Ajax was happy. He was in his office muttering *"Beak like a broad-head spear—The Elephant Bird, the Elephant Bird—Had nobody else to . . ."*

Here's a photograph Mark took of Ajax trying to figure out what the last word of the second verse of "The Elephant Bird" should be. He called it "The Thinker."

"The Thinker," by Mark Maxwell.

(This photograph, by the way, was so good—as you can see—that Ajax later used it on the back cover of his book. It is reprinted here with Mark's permission and a fee of four dollars.)

Happy too was Aunt Susan Standish. She was upstairs making the soft, happy sounds a person who has on a white satin sleeping mask makes when she or he is having a good dream.

And Mark was happy. He was wandering around the house taking pictures of everyone else. And taking pictures of everyone else was what made Mark happiest.

chapter 25

In Which We Resume Our Story Where We Left Off, Before All That Business About Hums

"Where's the note *from Ms. Killingher, Moxy?"* Mrs. Maxwell said again. She said it so loudly that the hum in the house turned into a buzz.

"Note?" said Moxy casually. She said it as if someone had asked her to pass the salt. "Oh, you must mean the note from Ms. Killingher. It's got to be here somewhere."

chapter 26
In Which Moxy Tries to Remember Where She Put the Note

Moxy called out to her stepfather. "Ajax?" she said. "Did I give you that note Ms. Killingher sent home with me while Mother was in Africa?"

"The Elephant Bird, the Elephant Bird had nobody else to . . . Had nobody else to . . . Had nobody else to—"

"Hello, Ajax," said Moxy. Suddenly she was standing in his doorway.

"The Elephant Bird, the Elephant Bird had nobody else to . . . Had nobody else to . . . Had nobody else to—"

"I'm sorry, darling," interrupted Mrs. Maxwell. Now *she* was standing in the doorway next to Moxy. "I know your editor expected 'The Elephant Bird' yesterday. And you've been so understanding—taking complete care of the children and the house and everything else while I dashed off to Africa at the last minute. But Moxy is under the impression she gave you a note from Ms. Killingher last week."

"Note?" said Ajax. He had heard the word recently—he just couldn't remember where.

"I'm not absolutely, positively, one hundred percent certain I gave it to him," said Moxy.

Mrs. Maxwell looked at her sharply. "Yes or no?" she said.

"Possibly," said Moxy.

chapter 27
In Which There Is
a Surprise

Here is the surprise: Pansy arrived.

"I found *the note!*" she cried.

Pansy had been hanging out halfway down and halfway up the stairs when she heard Mrs. Maxwell ask Moxy where the note was. It had been easy for Pansy to find the note because Pansy *had* the note. Pansy kept everything Moxy lost, in case Moxy couldn't find it.

For her part, Moxy was in shock—she was sure she'd lost the note way better than that.

Pansy proudly presented the envelope with the note in it to Mrs. Maxwell.

. . . and THE ENVELOPE, please.

It was very scary. The letters alone, as you can see from the photograph Mark took, were quite black and thick, and the penmanship was nothing less than excellent. Even Mrs. Maxwell was nervous about opening it.

chapter 29
In Which We Learn
What Was *Inside*
THE ENVELOPE

Inside **THE ENVELOPE** was *the note.*

chapter 30
In Which We Learn
What the Note Said

Let us read the note silently to ourselves as Mrs. Maxwell reads aloud:

Dear Mrs. Maxwell,

I regret to inform you that your daughter Moxy A. Maxwell does not stop playing "Heart and Soul" when she reaches the end. She just plays on and on. Unpleasant news to your ears, no doubt, but there it is.

I don't think it would be fair to the rest of my students to include her in the recital if she can't play the song the way it's meant to be played.

It is very important that Moxy practice hard at stopping this week.

After all, the Killingher School for Piano and Bass must maintain the standard of excellence it has come to represent to this entire community—indeed, this entire suburb!

I have always believed that practice makes perfect, but in the case of Moxy, I may be wrong.

Regretfully,
Corinne Killingher

P.S. Would you also please see if you can do something about the pounding?

"Moxy," said Mrs. Maxwell, "*do you stop playing 'Heart and Soul' when you reach the end?*"

"Well, 'Heart and Soul' is such a short

song," said Moxy. "If I play it the regular way it doesn't give me much time to be onstage."

"Moxy, *will* you *stop* playing your part of 'Heart and Soul' when you get to the end tonight?" asked Mrs. Maxwell.

chapter 31
In Which, for the Second Time in Three Books, Moxy Is Saved by the Bell

"Saved by the bell" means the phone rings just as you're trying to think of a good answer for a tough question.

Then the phone rang. And Mrs. Maxwell, who was so close to it that the left ear of her right bunny slipper was flopped over the receiver, answered.

"Hello," managed Mrs. Maxwell.

It was Ms. Killingher.

Mrs. Maxwell slid down the hall wall and came to a stop, stooping on her bunny slippers.

Instead of saying "Hello," Ms. Killingher said, "We must have been disconnected."

"I'm very sorry," said Mrs. Maxwell. "But I just read the note. You see, I've been in Africa all week taking care of my sister. She fell off a ladder while she was feeding a giraffe."

Mrs. Maxwell definitely sounded like Moxy, thought Ms. Killingher, not for the first time. Moxy often had odd reasons for not practicing the piano.

Naturally, Ms. Killingher said how sorry she was to hear about Mrs. Maxwell's sister. And that she hoped she was on the mend. And all the sorts of things you say when someone's sister has fallen off a ladder while feeding a giraffe.

Then Ms. Killingher said, "Will Moxy be able to stop playing her part of 'Heart and Soul' when she reaches the end tonight?"

chapter 32
The Moment of Truth

Mrs. Maxwell put her hand over the mouthpiece of the phone and said, "Ms. Killingher wants to know if you'll stop playing your part of 'Heart and Soul' when you get to the end tonight."

"Yes," said Moxy, *"but—"*

But before Moxy could say *"but I've never done it before,"* her mother said, "She will!" to Ms. Killingher, thus putting an end to this chapter.

chapter 33
Trouble

"Well then...," said Mrs. Maxwell after she hung up with Ms. Killingher.

"Well then," Moxy sighed, "I guess I'd better get out there." Moxy pointed toward the front porch.

"You aren't going anywhere," said Mrs. Maxwell, "until I've heard you and Pansy play 'Heart and Soul' the way it's supposed to be played."

"But we can't play 'Heart and Soul' until the Big Dress Rehearsal."

Moxy had experience with dress rehearsals. When she played the part of

63

Cottage Cheese in her second-grade Food Group play, they'd had a dress rehearsal just before the actual performance. And everyone had to put on their costumes. Then they practiced the whole play. Just as if the audience were in the room.

"Let's have the dress rehearsal now!" said Mrs. Maxwell.

"But our outfits aren't ready," said Moxy. "We can't have a *real* dress rehearsal without them."

"Of course they're ready," replied Mrs. Maxwell. "I had your pink gobs-of-glitter dress pressed before I left. And Pansy's yellow buttercup dress is in the hall closet."

"I don't mean our *dresses*," said Moxy. "I mean the Surprise Part of our outfits."

Mrs. Maxwell yawned. "When will the Surprise Part of your outfits be ready?" she asked.

It was an excellent question as far as

Moxy was concerned. It meant she got to go out on the porch and ask Granny George when the capes they had been working on all week would be done, which meant she got to leave the room.

"I'll go ask Granny George," said Moxy.

chapter 34
In Which Moxy Arrives on the Porch Just in Time to Stop Granny George from Finishing the Capes

Granny George didn't need an extension cord for her sewing machine. That's because it didn't run on electricity. It ran on Granny George's foot. So when Moxy walked out onto the porch and tapped Granny George on the left shoulder, Granny George took her right foot off the pedal and the sewing machine stopped.

"The cape is smashing," Moxy said to Granny George. "May I try it on?"

chapter 35
In Which Moxy Is Grateful to Herself for Being So Thorough

The moment she put the cape on, Moxy was glad she'd taken the time to do it—because two things were wrong:

1. The gold glitter that spelled out Moxy's name in big letters across the back was starting to flake off.

2. Now that it was almost done, Moxy could tell that the whole thing would benefit from a bit of ermine fur trim.

In case you don't know what real ermine fur trim looks like, here is a photograph of the *real* Miss America cape so you can see for yourself. The girl in the picture is Moxy's great-great-grandmother. She is standing on a crate. Her name was also Moxy, by the way.

chapter 36
In Which Mark Delivers a Surprising Message for Moxy

Just then Mark came out on the porch with a surprising message for Moxy.

"Mom wants you to start practicing 'Heart and Soul'—*now!*" he said.

But Moxy wasn't listening—she was mulling. She was mulling over the ermine fur problem. You see, Moxy believed it was wrong to hurt animals in order to make fur coats. The problem was that Moxy liked the ermine fur *look*. What she was trying to figure out now was how to find seven or eight yards of high-quality *fake* ermine fur this late in the day.

chapter 37

In Which Pansy Follows Mark Out to the Porch

"Mom said you have to get in there and play 'Heart and Soul' *now*," said Pansy when she stepped out on the porch. Pansy's eyes were open very wide, though not quite as wide as saucers. They looked more like— no, they looked *exactly* like this picture Mark took of her:

"Eyes Not As Wide As Saucers," by *Mark Maxwell.*

But Moxy wasn't listening. Moxy wasn't listening because she had just had an *important breakthrough idea* about how to manufacture fake ermine fur this late in the day. And it is a well-established fact that when Moxy Maxwell is having an *important breakthrough idea*, she can't think of anything else.

chapter 38
What Moxy Did Next

"Pansy," Moxy said, "would you please run in and get the permanent black Magic Marker off Ajax's desk? Oh, and on your way back, would you mind grabbing your pink paper-doll scissors?

"And Mark," continued Moxy, "would you please go up to the guest room bathroom and get two of the old white guest towels and bring them down here ASAP?"

Pansy nodded, but her mouth said, "But Mom says we have to play 'Heart and Soul' *now*."

chapter 39
Which Begins:
Suddenly Mudd Was
Barking

Suddenly Mudd was barking.

Mudd was Moxy's very nice, not too
bright, part German shepherd, part Lab,
and part himself dog, and he was
barking and
barking and barking and
barking and barking
barking and barking and barking
barking and barking and barking
and barking and barking and barking and barking and barking and barking
and barking and barking and barking and barking and barking and barking and
and   barking and barking and barking and barking and barking and barking and barking
and barking and barking and barking and barking and barking and barking and barking and
and barking and barking and barking and barking and barking and barking and barking
barking and barking and barking and barking and barking and barking and
barking and barking and barking and barking and barking and barking
and barking and barking and barking and barking and barking and
barking and barking and   barking and barking and barking
barking and   and barking
and barking   barking and
and barking and   barking
barking and   barking
and   barking   barking
and   barking   barking
barking   barking and
barking   and
barking.

"Stop barking!" commanded Moxy.

And
barking and
barking and barking and
barking and barking
barking and barking and barking
barking and barking and barking
and barking and barking and barking and barking and barking and barking
and barking and barking and barking and barking and barking and barking and
and barking and barking and barking and barking and barking and barking and barking
and barking and barking and barking and barking and barking and barking and barking and
and barking and barking and barking and barking and barking and barking and barking
barking and barking and barking and barking and barking and barking and
barking and barking and barking and barking and barking and barking
and barking and barking and barking and barking and barking and
barking and barking and   barking and barking and barking
barking and   and barking
and barking   barking and
and barking and   barking
barking and   barking
and barking   barking
and barking   barking
barking   barking and
barking   and
    barking.

The reason Mudd was barking was that he wanted everyone to know that Sam was standing outside the porch door.

"Sam! Thank goodness you're here!" Moxy called out.

"Is that your cape?" said Sam.

Moxy twirled around a couple of times so that Sam could admire it.

"Some of the glitter is coming off," said Sam. He was only six. But he paid such close attention to details that you would have thought he was seven.

"It just needs a little fake ermine fur trim and it will be *très élégante*," replied Moxy. (Mark had been teaching Moxy a new French word every day for the last three days and now she was almost 100% bilingual. She could work "*très*" and "*oui*" and "*non*" into almost any English sentence.)

"Have you had the Big Dress Rehearsal yet?" said Sam. Sam was a little worried. Each time Moxy practiced the piano, she played her part of "Heart and Soul" over and over. She never seemed to reach the end.

"I can't start the Big Dress Rehearsal until our capes are ready," said Moxy. "And our capes won't be ready until they have a little fake ermine fur trim on them. And I can't start making the fake ermine fur trim until

Mark gets the old white towels from the guest room bathroom. And Pansy gets her pink paper-doll scissors and Ajax's permanent black Magic Marker."

"I'll get the old white guest towels," offered Sam.

"I'll help," said Pansy.

Mark said nothing.

"Thank you," said Moxy. "But please be very quiet when you go up. We don't want to wake Aunt Susan Standish."

"Aunt Susan Standish is *here*?" said Sam.

Moxy nodded solemnly. Sam had met Aunt Susan Standish once. She reminded him of how Moxy would be when she grew up. Neither of them seemed afraid of anything.

chapter 40
In Which Pansy and Sam Run into Mrs. Maxwell's Sun

When Pansy and Sam turned to go back inside, they found themselves face to face with the orange sun rising behind Mrs. Maxwell's SMILE, YOU'RE IN MIAMI sweatshirt.

"Excuse us," said Pansy without looking up.

Mrs. Maxwell stepped one step to her left. And Sam and Pansy stepped one step to *their* left and disappeared into the house.

chapter 41
In Which Moxy Almost Cries

"What's that?" Mrs. Maxwell said sharply.

"What's what?" said Moxy.

"What you're wearing."

Moxy looked down at her cape—she had forgotten she had it on.

"Please don't look!" cried Moxy. But her mother didn't look away. So Moxy was forced to toss the back of the cape over her head—even though it hurt her neck—so her mother couldn't see it.

Here is the photograph Mark took of

Moxy hiding her face under her cape. He called it "My Sister Looks Better with a Cape Over Her Face."

"My Sister Looks Better with a Cape Over Her Face," by Mark Maxwell.

"Moxy, I am too tired to play games!" said Mrs. Maxwell. "If you and Pansy aren't in that house playing 'Heart and Soul' all the way through by the time I count to ten, there are going to be consequences."

(Mrs. Maxwell always counted to whatever age you were before she took action. Moxy could hardly wait until she was 100.)

But Moxy didn't reply. Somewhere under her black velvet cape it sounded like she was starting to cry.

"Darling," said Mrs. Maxwell, "are you crying?"

"No," said Moxy, "I'm sighing. It was supposed to be a surprise!"

"What was supposed to be a surprise?"

"This," said Moxy, flipping the cape from her head. "And it's not even finished yet!"

"But it *is* a surprise," said Mrs. Maxwell, looking at the cape. "What is it for?"

"It's for me to wear tonight," said Moxy. "Pansy has one too. But we haven't even started to make the fake ermine fur trim yet."

The porch swing was damp and covered with a light dusting of mud from the melted snow. It was also covered with seventy-nine straight pins that had spilled from Granny George's straight pin container. But Mrs. Maxwell sat down anyway. Mrs. Maxwell really needed to sit down.

"I thought you were wearing the pink gobs-of-glitter dress tonight," she said. She pulled a pair of straight pins from under her right thigh.

"I *am* wearing the pink gobs-of-glitter dress. But the cape goes over it."

"For the recital?"

"And a crown, of course."

"Of course," repeated Mrs. Maxwell.

"And my silver tap shoes."

"I see," said Mrs. Maxwell, who did.

chapter 42
In Which
Mrs. Maxwell's Eyes
Take a Little Rest

The swing was stirring in the slight (5 mph) breeze coming from the northeast. It was very restful. Mrs. Maxwell did not so much close her eyes as her eyes closed on Mrs. Maxwell.

Let us remember that Mrs. Maxwell had been up all night flying from Africa to Cleveland—it took twenty-one hours and two minutes. And she hadn't had any sleep. And when she got home she didn't go to bed. She stayed up to make 150 cupcakes with marshmallow frosting for Moxy's party tonight.

Not that she was sleeping now, Mrs. Maxwell reassured herself. She didn't have time to sleep. She had to make sure Moxy could stop playing her part of "Heart and Soul" because . . . because . . . because. Suddenly Mrs. Maxwell couldn't remember why it was so important to hear Moxy stop playing "Heart and Soul."

The reason Mrs. Maxwell couldn't remember why it was so important to hear Moxy practice "Heart and Soul" was because Mrs. Maxwell had fallen asleep. In fact, she was already dreaming. She was dreaming there was a giraffe in the upstairs shower. It was singing "Heart and Soul."

When Moxy realized that her mother was asleep, she took some of the leftover velvet from the capes Granny George had made and covered her mother with it so she wouldn't get cold, even though there was only a slight (5 mph) breeze.

chapter 43
In Which the Word "Intermission" Is Explained

An Intermission is when you, the Reader, take a break from reading this book. Not a long break. You can't, for example, go to Paris (unless of course you're already in Paris). But you can get up and get some gum. Or pet the dog. Or call a friend who is also reading this book, to see if they've gotten to the Intermission Part yet. But then you must come back. Because the story is just heating up. . . .

THE
INTERMISSION
PART

chapter 44
In Which
Mrs. Maxwell Wakes

The sound of Moxy and Pansy practicing "Heart and Soul" did not wake Mrs. Maxwell. What woke Mrs. Maxwell was the vibration of Granny George's sewing machine.

The reason the sound of Moxy and Pansy practicing "Heart and Soul" did not wake Mrs. Maxwell was that Moxy and Pansy were not practicing "Heart and Soul." They were upstairs in the guest room bathroom watching Sam cut the last white bath towel into five-inch strips with *the sharp scissors.*

In Which the Author Repeats the Phrase "with *the sharp scissors*"

With *the sharp scissors*.

In Which Mrs. Maxwell Yawns and Asks That Age-old Question: "How Long Have I Been Asleep?"

Out on the porch, Mrs. Maxwell yawned and asked Granny George that age-old question: "How long have I been asleep?"

"Two hours and twenty-one minutes," said Granny George. Granny George paid very close attention to time.

Mrs. Maxwell had also been asleep long enough for Moxy to have almost finished making the fake ermine fur trim out of the old white guest towels.

In fact, at the very moment when Mrs.

Maxwell was yawning on the swing, Moxy was perched on the edge of the pink sink in the guest bathroom. She was watching Pansy put black dots on the second-to-last strip of what had recently been a whole white towel. Pansy was using Ajax's permanent black Magic Marker.

For his part, Mark was taking this picture of Sam cutting the last towel into five-inch strips with, as I say (and it bears repeating), *the sharp scissors.*

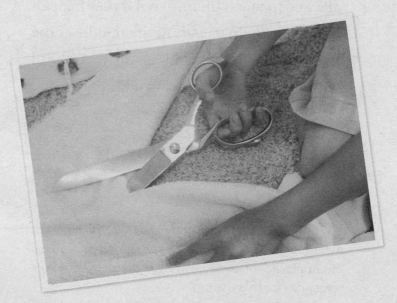

chapter 47
The Sharp Scissors—
a User's Guide

The sharp scissors are so sharp that children under the age of eighteen are not allowed to touch them—*even* if they happen to find *the sharp scissors* in the middle of the living room floor standing on their head with the sharp end sticking up.*

*WARNING: Children under the age of eighteen who touch *the sharp scissors* are subject to a maximum penalty of coming straight home from school every day for five years.

chapter 48

The Ins and Outs of High-Quality Fake Ermine Fur Manufacturing OR What Exactly Moxy Was Doing

Shall I go into detail about how to make high-quality fake ermine fur out of white bathroom towels? Or is it so obvious it would be a bore? If you already know how to make fake ermine fur trim out of white guest towels, please skip this chapter and go to Chapter 49.

Moxy Maxwell's last-minute, high-quality fake ermine fur recipe:

What you'll need:
1. Two old white towels.
2. One big (really fresh) permanent black Magic Marker.
3. One pair *sharp scissors* or small sword.
4. Granny George.

DIRECTIONS:
- Say "Please" and then ask someone to cut the white fluffy towel into long strips, perhaps 5 inches wide— perhaps more, perhaps less.
- Say "Please" again and ask someone to make big black dots all over the strips of the old white towels using the permanent black Magic Marker.
- Ask Granny George to please sew the black-and-white dotted strips of

bathroom towels around the outside of the capes.

- Add more dots as needed.

Yield: Enough ermine for two regular capes.

chapter 49

The Part of the Story in Which Mrs. Maxwell Begins to Climb Slooooowly Up the Stairs to Find Out Why Moxy Hasn't Started the Big Dress Rehearsal

Sloooooooooooooooooooooooooooo-
oooooooooooooooooooooooooooooo-
oooooooooooooooooooooooooooooo-
oooooooooooooooooooooooooooooo-
ooooooooooooooooooooooooowly,

                                    by step.

                              by step

                           by step

                        by step

                     by step

                  by step

               by step

            by step

         by step

      step

she climbed

chapter 50
Bad Times
OR
Moxy's Mother
Arrives

Here is a picture Mark took of what Mrs. Maxwell saw when she finally reached the bathroom door. He called it "A Shot of Chaos."

"A Shot of Chaos," by Mark Maxwell.

"Sam, put *the sharp scissors* down now!" cried Mrs. Maxwell.

It's a good thing that Sam had great reflexes and a lot of common sense. Otherwise, he might have cut himself when he heard Mrs. Maxwell's voice behind him. Instead, he stopped cutting.

"Now turn slowly around," instructed Mrs. Maxwell.

Sam turned slowly around, keeping *the sharp scissors* in clear view of everyone.

"Easy now, Sam," said Mrs. Maxwell as she approached him.

When she was absolutely sure Sam wouldn't make a sudden move, Mrs. Maxwell took *the sharp scissors* from him.

Then she sat down on the edge of the pink guest-room bathroom tub.

"I'm sorry," whispered Pansy. She was apologizing as much to Moxy as to her mother.

She was apologizing to Moxy because she had heard their mom coming up the stairs and she hadn't warned Moxy. Pansy hadn't warned Moxy because her heart had been bouncing around in her chest like a cartoon heart. And she had been afraid that if she opened her mouth, it might come bouncing out.

"I'm sorry too," said Sam. Sam was very good with mothers.

chapter 51

In Which Moxy (Almost) Takes the Blame

"It wasn't his fault," said Moxy. "I mean [there was a slight pause], *I'm* the one who told Sam to get *the sharp scissors*."

Mrs. Maxwell was suddenly alert. "Are you saying it was *your* fault?"

"Pansy's pink paper-doll scissors wouldn't cut the towels," said Moxy.

"So it's Pansy's paper-doll scissors' fault that you had to use *the sharp scissors*?"

"No, it was Sam who used *the sharp scissors*."

"But it's not his fault?"

"No, I told him to." Moxy was getting the teeny-tiniest bit impatient.

"You *do* know what happens to some-one who touches *the sharp scissors*," said Mrs. Maxwell.

"Five years," moaned Pansy.

Mrs. Maxwell looked at the mess on the bathroom floor. Then she looked at Moxy. "What are you doing up here anyway?" she said. "You and Pansy are supposed to be downstairs practicing 'Heart and Soul.' "

"I know," said Moxy. "But we can't have the Big Dress Rehearsal until our capes are ready."

"Yes, you can," said Mrs. Maxwell. Her voice had a *right now or else* quality to it.

"Maybe we can," Pansy suggested to Moxy.

chapter 52
In Which the Word "Spit" Appears

Mrs. Maxwell looked at Pansy for the first time. "What's on your face?" she said.

"My smile?" said Pansy hopefully.

"No, those black spots."

"They're ermine dots," said Moxy.

Mrs. Maxwell pulled a crumpled Kleenex from between her wrist and the elastic on her SMILE, YOU'RE IN MIAMI sweatshirt. Fortunately for Pansy, the Kleenex was clean.

"Come here," she said to Pansy.

Pansy moved almost an inch toward her.

"Closer," said Mrs. Maxwell.

When Pansy didn't move, Mrs. Maxwell

said, "Well, I'm not going to eat you," and reached out and pulled Pansy to her.

And yes, Reader, even though there was running water on two sides of her, Mrs. Maxwell licked the Kleenex and tried to wipe the black ermine dots off Pansy's face with her spit.

Then Mark took this picture.

"*Mother Attacks Child with Her Own Spit!*," by Mark Maxwell.

chapter 53
In Which
Mrs. Maxwell Gets
Back to the Point

Mrs. Maxwell sighed. Then she said, "Who gave you permission to use *the sharp scissors* anyway?"

"I did," said Aunt Susan Standish.

chapter 54
In Which We Meet Aunt Susan Standish When She's Awake

Aunt Susan Standish was leaning casually against the bathroom door. Her white satin sleeping mask was propped on top of her head like a pair of sunglasses. Her pajamas were made from the same white satin as her mask—the pajama legs fell fashionably just below the knee. The pajama top had three-quarter-length sleeves.

Even when she slept, Aunt Susan Standish was *très élégante*, thought Moxy. In fact, if Aunt Susan Standish hadn't been wearing a pair of green wool knee socks with a hole in the left big toe, you never

104

would have known that Aunt Susan Standish was Moxy's mother's twin sister.

"Mind if I sit down?" said Aunt Susan Standish.

Mrs. Maxwell slid over so her sister could sit beside her on the edge of the tub.

Here is a picture Mark took of Aunt Susan Standish's green wool knee sock with the hole in the big toe sitting next to Mrs. Maxwell's right bunny slipper with the Green Grass Power Shake powder on it. He called it "The Sisters Go Toe to Toe."

"The Sisters Go Toe to Toe," by Mark Maxwell.

"You told Moxy she could use *the sharp scissors?*" said Mrs. Maxwell.

"I believe so," said Aunt Susan Standish.

"But I thought you were asleep," said Mrs. Maxwell.

"I was," said Aunt Susan Standish.

"Then how could you give Moxy permission to use *the sharp scissors?*"

"Aunt Susan Standish can talk in her sleep," said Pansy.

Aunt Susan Standish stretched and then yawned. "I'm feeling much better," she said. "Hello, everyone!" she added as she pulled out of a second yawn. Then she looked at her sister. Then she stretched again. And since her arm was already out there, she reached over and patted the top of Mrs. Maxwell's head.

"Hello, sweet sister," Aunt Susan Standish said. "You must be tired."

"Actually," said Mrs. Maxwell, "I'm counting to ten. One . . ."

Moxy was shocked. Her mother was more awake than she'd thought.

"Two . . . if you girls aren't down at that piano playing 'Heart and Soul' by the time I'm through . . . three . . . there are going to be consequences."

It was hard for Moxy to imagine what could be worse than coming straight home every day after school for the next five years.

"Four . . ." Mrs. Maxwell was definitely getting her Mother Strength back.

"What consequences?" said Pansy.

"Five . . . ," replied Mrs. Maxwell. "Six . . . If you aren't downstairs playing 'Heart and Soul' by the time I've finished counting to ten—seven . . . ," said Mrs. Maxwell, "I'm going to call Ms. Killingher and tell her you can't be in the recital."

"Eight" was the last thing Moxy and Pansy and Sam heard as they disappeared down the stairs.

chapter 55
A Few Statistics About the Duet Moxy and Pansy Are About to Play

Here is what you, the Reader, need to know before Moxy and Pansy start playing their recital piece:

    1. It is called "Heart and Soul."

    2. Moxy's part starts a little while after Pansy's part.

    3. Moxy's part is really really really really *really* hard.

chapter 56
In Which Sam
Is Helpful

As soon as they got downstairs, Moxy said, "Sam, would you please play my part of 'Heart and Soul'? I have to run out to the porch and give Granny George this last strip of fake ermine fur guest towel trim so she can finish our capes in time for us to wear them for the Big Dress Rehearsal."

"Sure," said Sam.

Sam knew how to play "Heart and Soul." He had learned it in case Moxy needed help.

"What if Mom comes down?" said Pansy.

But Moxy had already gone out to the porch.

As soon as Sam started playing Moxy's part of "Heart and Soul," Ajax drifted out from his office to see what was up. He'd never heard Moxy play her part so well.

chapter 57
In Which We See Mrs. Maxwell on the Top Step with Her Head Against the Wall and Her Eyes Closed, Listening to "Heart and Soul"

"A Study of a Sleeping Mother," by Mark Maxwell.

chapter 58
In Which Moxy Comes Back into the House but Without the Capes

"The capes are almost ready," announced Moxy as she came in from the porch. "You're doing a very good job playing my part of 'Heart and Soul,' Sam," she added. She listened for a few seconds to see if she could figure out how Sam was going to finish it.

"The crowns!" cried Moxy suddenly. "I almost forgot about the crowns. We can't have a *real* dress rehearsal without them."

Sam didn't stop playing Moxy's part of "Heart and Soul," though he did nod in the direction of the stairs. "But your mom is up there," he said.

"But she's in the bathroom talking to Aunt Susan Standish," said Moxy.

"Don't forget our silver tap shoes!" Pansy called out as Moxy started up the stairs.

chapter 59
Dark at the Top of the Stairs

Most people would have stopped if they had seen their mother sitting slumped against the hall wall at the top of the stairs. But Moxy felt it was probably very good for her mother to have a little nap, so she carefully stepped around her.

chapter 60
Dark at the Top of the Stairs—Part II

Unfortunately, it was not quite dark enough at the top of the stairs, because just as Moxy was walking by, Mrs. Maxwell opened her eyes and looked at Moxy in surprise.

At first Mrs. Maxwell was confused. She could hear Moxy playing her part of "Heart and Soul" downstairs. Yet there was Moxy standing in front of her.

"Who," said Mrs. Maxwell, "is playing your part of 'Heart and Soul'?"

chapter 61

In Which Aunt Susan Standish Enters in What Is Known as the Nick of Time

"You were playing the piano beautifully," Aunt Susan Standish said to Moxy. "But who is playing it now?"

"Sam," said Moxy quietly.

Mrs. Maxwell was quite calm.

The fact that her mother was quite calm worried Moxy a great deal, I don't mind telling you.

Then Mrs. Maxwell stood up (with the assistance of the railing and her sister) and said to Aunt Susan Standish, "Would you care to join me? I'm going downstairs to hear Moxy play her part of 'Heart and Soul.' "

Aunt Susan Standish said she'd be delighted. And the three walked down the dark stairs.

chapter 62

Whose Title Is "As Soon As Moxy Sat Down at the Piano"

"Fear!" shouted Ajax as soon as Moxy sat down at the piano. Ajax got up from his chair. "Fear! Fear! Fear!" he cried.

Everyone looked over at him—except for Granny George, who was still out on the porch finishing the capes.

"Dear," said Mrs. Maxwell, going over to her husband, "are you okay?"

"Of course!" said Ajax, thumping his forehead with his hand. "Why didn't I see it before? *FEAR!* It's the perfect word to rhyme with 'spear.'"

"I must write it down," he said. He practically ran from the room.

As soon as Ajax practically ran from the room, Mudd started to bark. (Mudd always barked when Moxy sat down to play the piano. That was because Moxy played her part so loudly.)

As soon as Mudd started to bark, Moxy got up, walked slowly over to the porch door, and let him out.

As soon as Moxy let Mudd out, she sat back down at the piano.

As soon as Moxy sat back down at the piano, her mother sat down next to her. Moxy looked up at her mother. "Mother," she said, "would you please move over? Your hip is practically touching my shoulder."

Mrs. Maxwell moved her hip one inch.

"Begin," said Mrs. Maxwell.

Pansy began to play.

But when Moxy didn't join in, Pansy stopped.

As soon as Pansy stopped, Granny George hurried in from the porch. The capes were in her arms.

"Wait!" called out Granny George.

Then she draped one cape over Moxy's shoulders and the other over Pansy's. "Sorry to interrupt," she added. She crept over to the sofa and sat down next to her daughter (who was also Aunt Susan Standish).

"Continue," said Mrs. Maxwell.

"Now we have to start all over," sighed Moxy. "Play it again, Pansy."

chapter 63
In Which "Heart and Soul" Begins and Ends

Reader, I wish a CD came with this book. That way you could hear for yourself what Mark and Sam and Mrs. Maxwell and Aunt Susan Standish and Granny George heard when Moxy played her part of "Heart and Soul." But it's probably just as well.

Moxy's song went on so long that finally Mrs. Maxwell had to tap her on the shoulder.

"You can stop now," said Mrs. Maxwell.

As soon as Mrs. Maxwell said she could stop, Moxy and Pansy got up and walked to the middle of the living room. Then they held their hands together in the air the way heavyweight champions do and bowed and bowed. It was Moxy's favorite part of the whole show. She and Pansy had rehearsed it at least a hundred times last week.

"You may clap now," said Moxy.

Everyone clapped.

chapter 64
In Which Mrs. Maxwell Makes a Comment or Two About the Song

"How very . . . ," said Mrs. Maxwell— she paused to think about it—"long. And what was all that pounding about?"

"That was the sound of the heart," said Moxy.

"It was pretty loud," noted Mrs. Maxwell. "And it never stopped," she added.

"Well, a heart's not supposed to stop," said Moxy. "Unless of course it's dead, and my heart isn't."

"No," said Mrs. Maxwell quietly, "it isn't."

Moxy sat down in the rocking chair. She was tired. Playing "Heart and Soul" was hard work.

"Moxy," said Mrs. Maxwell, "will you promise to stop playing 'Heart and Soul' tonight when you get to the end?"

"Of course," said Moxy. "I mean, I can't play all night. Other people have to play after me."

"People like me," said Mark, who was now sitting at the piano bench.

"Maybe Mark should practice while I go upstairs and warm up my voice. Ms. Killingher still might ask me to sing tonight," said Moxy.

But Mrs. Maxwell was not convinced that Moxy would stop playing the piano.

"Pansy," said Mrs. Maxwell, "can you stop playing the piano when your part is through?"

Pansy nodded.

"Moxy, will you promise to stop when Pansy stops?"

"But that will make it so short," said Moxy.

"Promise?" said Mrs. Maxwell.

Moxy really thought about it. "I'll do my best," she said.

It was all Mrs. Maxwell could ask—all anyone can ask of anyone.

chapter 65

In Which Mark Plays "The Flight of the Bumblebee" Perfectly and We Learn a Little About Stage Makeup

While Mark practiced, Moxy, Sam, and Pansy went upstairs to finish getting ready. Unfortunately, there wasn't enough time to steam up her bathroom so Moxy could warm up her voice in case someone asked her to sing tonight. Instead, she sang "La la la la la la la la" over and over while she put on her stage makeup.

Moxy had stage makeup left over from when she played the part of Cottage Cheese last year in the Food Group play.

Stage makeup is very different from regular makeup. It is quite thick. And Moxy put on a little extra. Then she put some on Pansy. Then she put more on Pansy. But Moxy couldn't cover up the black ermine dots.

Before Moxy and Pansy could even practice walking with their capes and crowns and tap shoes on (all at the same time), Mrs. Maxwell called from downstairs to say it was time to go.

Walking down stairs in slippery, silvery, somewhat high, high-heeled tap shoes while wearing a crown that keeps falling down in front of your face with every step you take is not as easy as it may sound.

By the time Moxy and Pansy reached the downstairs hall, everyone was already waiting for them out in the car.

"But we can't go yet," Moxy called out from the porch.

Mrs. Maxwell turned on the ignition in reply.

"Mark still has to take the picture of me standing in front of the trees with my cape and crown on!" shouted Moxy. "It's for my Christmas card. I'm sending out my own this year."

When Mrs. Maxwell still didn't turn off the car, Moxy wobbled down the porch steps and over to her mother's side of the car. Mrs. Maxwell rolled down the window.

"I'm going to look just like Great-great-granny Moxy in that picture of her in the Miss America cape," said Moxy.

Mrs. Maxwell turned off the ignition.

Here is the picture Mark took of Moxy wearing her own ermine, towel-trimmed cape. You can hardly see the cardboard box she's standing on. She looks a lot like Great-great-granny Moxy, don't you think?

chapter 66
In Which Mrs. Maxwell Drives Their 1989 Volvo DL Station Wagon to the Palace Theater

Everyone piled into the car. Granny George was in the front seat. She was sitting between Mrs. Maxwell and Ajax. Ajax was reciting the second verse of his poem aloud. He was very proud and not a little relieved to have found the perfect word to rhyme with "spear."

> *"Claws as sharp as razor blades*
> *Beak like a broad-head spear*
> *The Elephant Bird, the Elephant Bird*
> *Had nobody else to fear!"*

Ajax put a little extra emphasis on the word "fear" at the very end, and Granny George started to applaud.

"No applause yet," said Ajax. "I still have to finish the last verse." Then he began to mutter something about sixty million years.

Sam and Mark were in the way back-seat. They were watching the front tires spatter slush from the melting snow. They were saying things like "neat" and "cool" and "nice one" whenever a big bunch of brown slush smacked the side of the car.

Aunt Susan Standish was sitting beside Pansy in the middle row of seats. Pansy's tap shoes were off: She was wearing them over her hands like gloves. When Ajax had finished his poem, Pansy had tapped her hands together for a very long time.

Moxy was on the other side of Pansy.

Before Ajax began his poem, she had been singing "La la la la la la la la la" to warm up her voice. And although she was happy that Ajax had found the perfect rhyme for "spear," she was not quite happy enough to applaud when he finally shouted out "fear!" at the end. Her stomach suddenly felt a little funny.

chapter 67
In Which Moxy Has
a Heart Attack

Mrs. Maxwell was just pulling into the parking lot of the Palace Theater in their 1989 Volvo DL station wagon when Moxy noticed that she was having a heart attack.

"Mother, I'm having a heart attack," said Moxy.

Moxy's mother said, "It's probably just nerves."

"What are nerves?" asked Moxy.

"It's like stage fright," said Granny George.

"Why would I be afraid of the stage?" said Moxy. "I love the stage."

After Mrs. Maxwell parked the car, she gave Mark and Moxy and Pansy a good-luck kiss. Then she and Ajax and Granny George and Aunt Susan Standish and Sam went into the main entrance of the Palace Theater.

Ms. Killingher had said that everyone performing in the recital should meet backstage. So Pansy and Mark and Moxy headed toward the back of the Palace Theater. Pansy was so excited she was running.

"Look, Moxy," called out Pansy. "It says STAGE next to the door. Just like you said it would!"

Even Mark was excited. Moxy could tell because he stopped and took a picture of the sign that said STAGE next to the door.

The Stage Door.

Moxy didn't seem to be as excited as Mark and Pansy. For one thing, she was not walking very quickly. In fact, when Mark was taking this picture of the stage door, Moxy was still back in the parking lot. Her stomach felt like it was purple inside.

"Moxy!" Pansy called out. "Hurry up!"

Slowly, Moxy hurried up—even though she didn't feel like it. As she watched her silver shoes tap across the parking lot, she wondered what made people do things they didn't want to do when there wasn't a mother around telling them to do it. Still, she was moving.

chapter 68
Backstage

AS soon as they got backstage and checked in with Ms. Killingher, Mark and Moxy pulled the big curtain back so they could see the audience. Aunt Susan Standish and their mother were standing together down in the front.

Everyone was admiring Aunt Susan Standish. She was wearing black kid gloves that reached all the way to her elbows and black very-high heels and sunglasses and a bright red swing coat with bell sleeves. Every time she turned to say hello to someone her coat moved in the opposite direction.

Mark took out the new super-duper-extra-extra-extra-strong telescopic lens that Aunt Susan Standish had brought him from Africa last Christmas. She said it was the kind of lens that *real* photographers used when they wanted to take a picture of the eye of a tiger out in the jungle. He screwed it onto his camera and took this very close close-up picture of Aunt Susan Standish from backstage.

"*Aunt Susan Standish Looking* Très Élégante," *by Mark Maxwell.*

The lens really worked. It got so close to Aunt Susan Standish that you could have counted her teeth if her mouth had been open.

Ajax and Sam were already sitting down. Granny George was between them.

Ajax was joyfully muttering to himself. He was working on the third and final verse of his elephant bird poem.

chapter 69

In Which the Average Reader Might Guess That Moxy Was Disappointed to Discover That Instead of the 2,400 People She Was Expecting to Be in the Audience, There Were Only 23

The average reader might guess that Moxy was disappointed to discover that instead of the 2,400 people she was expecting to be in the audience, there were only 23.

But Moxy wasn't all that disappointed. Her stomach felt purple. (If that's the word for it.)

Ms. Killingher told everyone backstage to gather round. She had an announcement. "People," said Ms. Killingher, "can I have your attention, please?"

Moxy and Pansy went tapping over. Mark followed.

"What are those?" said Ms. Killingher. She was pointing at the capes Moxy and Pansy were wearing.

"Our recital capes," said Pansy. "They match our crowns." Pansy put her crown on.

"Oh," said Ms. Killingher.

Then Ms. Killingher made her announcement. "The Curtain Person is having trouble remembering when the curtain is supposed to go up and when it's supposed to go down, so some of you may have to duck a little when you go out onstage." She looked at Moxy and Pansy's crowns. "Maybe you should leave them back here," she suggested. "They could fall off."

You might have expected Moxy to

protest. The crowns were, after all, an important part of the fabulous look that she had put together for tonight. But Moxy just put her crown carefully down on a nearby chair. Then she peeked through the curtain at the audience again. It looked like there were at least thirty people out there now. Her stomach still felt purple. And now her heart was beating hard.

Moxy had been sure there would be a vase with approximately 100 long-stemmed roses on top of the piano. But there was not. There was a goldfish bowl with one pink carnation floating around. She wasn't very upset, though. She was beginning to sweat in the place where her cape was tied around her neck.

chapter 70
In Which Elinor Hills plays "Twinkle, Twinkle, Little Star"

Ms. Killingher lined everyone up according to the order they were going to play in. Then she crossed her lips with her finger to remind everyone to be quiet. And the lights went down in the audience. And the lights came up on the stage. And Ms. Killingher walked out.

There was a lot of applause. Moxy thought it sounded like a lot more than thirty people were out there now. She grabbed Pansy's hand.

"Ladies and gentlemen," Ms. Killingher said into the microphone, "welcome to the

Killingher School of Piano and Bass's first annual recital."

Since Moxy and Pansy were third in line to go on, they were standing close to the stage. And they could see Ms. Killingher from the side. She looked very calm.

Moxy cleared her throat. She had hoped Ms. Killingher would ask her to sing tonight. Now she was hoping Ms. Killingher wouldn't. How could she sing when she could hardly swallow?

Ms. Killingher continued, "Elinor Hills will begin our concert. She will be playing 'Twinkle, Twinkle, Little Star.' Elinor?" And Elinor Hills walked out onstage.

As Ms. Killingher was walking off, she winked at Elinor. Elinor winked back. Then Elinor sat down at the piano and began playing "Twinkle, Twinkle, Little Star."

Moxy hadn't learned to wink yet, though teaching herself to wink was on her list of Ninety-nine Things to Learn before she turned thirteen. So Moxy wasn't sure what she'd do if Ms. Killingher winked at her when she went on. No one had told her she might have to wink tonight. Otherwise she would have learned to do it. It was something a person her age should know how to do.

And why was she thinking about winking anyhow? It was almost time for her to go on. But what should she be thinking about? She wasn't sure. *Maybe I should be wondering if I'll trip in my tap shoes*, thought Moxy. She knew she should have practiced that part. Her legs were beginning to shake. She picked her crown up off the chair and sat down.

Her hands were cold.

Or maybe, thought Moxy, *I should think about my part of "Heart and Soul" and what will happen if I forget how it goes.*

What if I forget how it goes?

What if I forget how it goes?

Moxy was having trouble breathing.

"Are you okay?" asked Pansy. Moxy's hand was freezing.

Moxy shook her head. "Pansy," she whispered, "get Mark."

But Mark was last in line. That's because "The Flight of the Bumblebee" was the hardest song to play.

chapter 71
In Which Elinor Hills Finishes Playing "Twinkle, Twinkle, Little Star"

In Moxy's humble opinion, Elinor Hills played "Twinkle, Twinkle, Little Star" far too quickly. It should have gone on for at least an hour—maybe more. But suddenly Elinor Hills was offstage and standing beside Moxy again. And Ms. Killingher was back onstage.

"How was it?" asked Moxy.

"It was brutal," said Elinor.

chapter 72
In Which
Joan DeMayo Plays
"Chopsticks"

"And now, Joan DeMayo, who has been a student here at the Killingher School of Piano and Bass for almost five months, will play 'Chopsticks,' " Ms. Killingher said to the audience. And Joan DeMayo, who had been standing in line in front of Moxy, trotted out onstage. She seemed very happy to go, thought Moxy. She was almost running.

Moxy couldn't tell if Ms. Killingher winked at Joan when Joan went out, because by then Moxy had put her head between her knees.

chapter 73
In Which
Mark Arrives

As soon as Mark arrived, he took this picture of Moxy with her head between her knees.

Then Mark knelt down. "What's wrong?" he whispered.

But Moxy didn't look up at him.

"I don't want to go on," mumbled Moxy.

"What!" exclaimed Mark. He said it so loudly that Ms. Killingher had to pretend to zip her lips to remind him to be quiet.

"But you love being the center of attention," whispered Mark.

"I think maybe . . . I might be . . . just possibly . . . I'm afraid."

"*You? Afraid?*" Mark had never heard Moxy say she was afraid of anything.

Moxy nodded. "I might be afraid I'll make a mistake." She said it very quietly and more to herself than to anyone else.

Mark looked at Moxy. She didn't look well. Her forehead was starting to sweat—even with all the stage makeup, you could still tell.

Pansy was looking up at him. "What's wrong with Moxy?" she whispered.

"She's afraid she might make a mistake," said Mark.

"But Moxy couldn't make a mistake," said Pansy.

chapter 74
In Which
Joan DeMayo
Finishes "Chopsticks"

Reader, if there is a faster song than
"Chopsticks" I don't know what it is. And
Joan DeMayo's interpretation of the beloved
tune was nearly electric. She was on- and
offstage in ninety seconds. Granny George
timed it.

chapter 75
In Which
Ms. Killingher
Announces That
Moxy and Pansy
Are Going to Play
"Heart and Soul"

Ms. Killingher sort of ran onstage (she hadn't expected Joan DeMayo to finish "Chopsticks" so quickly).

"And now for a duet!" Ms. Killingher said to the audience. "Moxy Maxwell and her sister, Pansy Maxwell, will play 'Heart and Soul.'"

The audience started to applaud. Ajax and Granny George and Aunt Susan Standish clapped very hard. Sam was even louder. Mrs. Maxwell was so nervous she forgot to clap. We all know what Mrs. Maxwell was nervous about. She was worried that Moxy would start to play "Heart and Soul" and never stop.

chapter 76
In Which
Moxy Maxwell and
Pansy Maxwell
Do Not Play
"Heart and Soul"

But Mrs. Maxwell didn't have to worry. She didn't have to worry because Moxy and Pansy didn't come out onstage.

When Moxy and Pansy didn't appear, there was a very loud silence in the audience. Then Ms. Killingher said again, "And now Pansy and Moxy Maxwell will play 'Heart and Soul.'"

chapter 77
In Which
Moxy Maxwell
and Pansy Maxwell
Do Not Play
"Heart and Soul" Again

Then, instead of Pansy and Moxy appearing onstage, Max Daks appeared onstage. Even though Max Daks was supposed to play right after Moxy, he could tell that Moxy didn't look very good. And he was worried that if Moxy and Pansy didn't get out there soon, the whole show might stop and he would lose his turn. Max Daks was planning to be a world-famous piano player by the time he was twelve. And he needed to practice playing in front of a live audience.

You could tell that Ms. Killingher was a little surprised to see Max Daks out there. But she remained calm when she said, "There's been a little mixup. It seems that instead of Moxy and Pansy, Max Daks will be playing . . ." Ms. Killingher checked the program she was holding. ". . . will be playing 'Glow, Little Glowworm, Glow.' " Ms. Killingher also forgot to wink at Max Daks when she rushed offstage.

"Moxy," said Ms. Killingher when she got backstage, "what's wrong? You and Pansy are supposed to be on."

"I want my mother," said Moxy. But Ms. Killingher couldn't hear her. Moxy's head was still between her knees.

"She wants our mom," Pansy explained to Ms. Killingher.

chapter 78
In Which Mrs. Maxwell Arrives Without Anyone Telling Her to Come

The moment Ms. Killingher announced that Moxy and Pansy were going to play "Heart and Soul" and Moxy and Pansy didn't come out onstage, Mrs. Maxwell got up from her seat, walked to the back of the Palace Theater, and went out the door. Then she walked through the parking lot and went in the stage door. That's because Mrs. Maxwell knew something was wrong— Moxy would never miss an entrance.

When Pansy saw her mom, she wasn't surprised. Her mom always came when *she* needed her.

"Mom," whispered Pansy, "Moxy's scared."

Moxy pulled her head from between her knees. She was so relieved to see her mother she almost started to cry.

Mrs. Maxwell knelt down and smoothed Moxy's hair. "What's wrong, darling?" she said quietly.

"I don't want to go out there," Moxy whispered.

Mrs. Maxwell had known Moxy for just over ten years now and she had never seen her like this. Moxy's hands were cold. And her legs were trembling. And white sweat was starting to streak from her forehead down her cheeks.

chapter 79
In Which
Aunt Susan Standish
Arrives

As soon as Aunt Susan Standish had
seen Mrs. Maxwell get up from her seat and
walk to the back of the Palace Theater, she
had followed her. A twin often knows when
something is wrong with the other twin.

chapter 80

In Which Moxy Sees Aunt Susan Standish

When Moxy looked up and saw Aunt Susan Standish standing behind her mother, she was so embarrassed, she put her head back between her knees.

"What's up?" said Aunt Susan Standish. Aunt Susan Standish did not whisper when she said it. But it didn't matter because Max Daks was making a lot of noise out there onstage.

"She doesn't want to go on," whispered Mrs. Maxwell.

"She's afraid," said Pansy helpfully.

"Well, of course she is!" said Aunt Susan Standish.

Moxy looked up. She hoped Aunt Susan Standish didn't think that she, Moxy Maxwell, was *always* afraid.

"She's afraid she might make a mistake," said Aunt Susan Standish.

"How did *you* know?" said Moxy.

"I'm a Mistake Expert. I'm always making mistakes," said Aunt Susan Standish. "The only reason I'm here is because I made a mistake."

"What do you mean?" said Moxy.

"If I hadn't been standing on a tippy ladder feeding a giraffe, I wouldn't have fallen off. If I hadn't fallen off, I wouldn't have gotten that concussion. If I hadn't gotten that concussion, your mother wouldn't have brought me to your house to stay. And if I hadn't been at your house, I wouldn't have been able to come to your recital today. I would hate to have missed all this."

"But what if I don't play?" mumbled Moxy.

But Aunt Susan Standish wasn't listening. "And last September I made a huge mistake. I took ten tourists on a shortcut through the rain forest. It took me two extra days to figure out where we were."

"Were you afraid?" interrupted Moxy.

"I would have been insane not to be," said Aunt Susan Standish.

"Then why did you take the shortcut?"

"Well, I was curious, I suppose, to find out where the shortcut would go." Aunt Susan Standish thought about it for a minute. Then she said, "I was more curious about where the shortcut would go than I was afraid of what would happen if I got lost."

"Moxy," said Mrs. Maxwell, "if you don't

want to go on, it's perfectly all right. We just have to make a decision."

Moxy closed her eyes. She wished she were young again and didn't have such hard decisions to make.

She knew that if she was afraid of going onstage now, she might always be afraid of going onstage. And if she was always afraid of going onstage, she would have to cross at least half the stuff off her list of 211 Possible Career Paths.

But what if she went onstage and made a mistake . . . what would she do?

Moxy turned to Mark. Mark was the smartest person she knew. "What will I do if I make a mistake?" she said.

"Do what you always do," said Mark. "Just keep on going."

Moxy remembered how earlier her feet had gone on walking across the parking lot toward the stage door even though the rest of her didn't want to go.

She remembered how nervous she'd been the first time she dove into the deep end of the pool when she was practicing her water ballet routine last summer. But it hadn't been that bad in the end (though the water had been surprisingly cold).

She remembered the time she sprayed Pansy's hair with gold spray paint and how afraid she'd been that her mother would kill her when she got home and saw what she'd done. But here she was—still alive.

Moxy could hear Max Daks playing the end of "Glow, Little Glowworm, Glow."

Moxy closed her eyes.

"Okay," she said, "I'll try."

Moxy surprised even herself when she said it.

chapter 81
On with the Show!

Max Daks was playing the end of "Glow, Little Glowworm, Glow" for the second time when Ms. Killingher tapped him on the shoulder. Not a person to stop in midmeasure, Max Daks finished the song.

As he was walking offstage, he heard Ms. Killingher say: "Ladies and gentlemen, at long last, Moxy and Pansy Maxwell will play 'Heart and Soul.' "

Reader, I wish I could say that Moxy's legs had stopped shaking. Or that her hands had warmed up and her heart wasn't beating like a bird in her chest. Or that her stomach didn't feel purple. But it wouldn't be true. In fact, Moxy's legs were shaking so much that her shoes were making extra little tapping sounds when she walked onstage.

But when the stage lights hit Moxy's eyes—the lights were bright blue on the sides and very white in the center—Moxy felt much better. The lights were so bright she couldn't see anyone in the audience. And the lights were warm. Their heat felt lovely on her hands.

After she sat down at the piano bench and just before she began, Moxy turned and looked at the lights again. For just a moment her eyes got lost in them. She felt like she was having a very pleasant dream. Then Pansy began to play her part of "Heart and Soul," and without hesitating Moxy joined her.

chapter 82

In Which We Learn How Moxy Sounded

Moxy's heart was pounding so loudly that she had to pound the piano even harder than usual to be sure she was playing "Heart and Soul" correctly.

Ms. Killingher, who was standing between Aunt Susan Standish and Moxy's mother, put her hands over her ears. She had never heard Moxy play so loudly before. Mrs. Maxwell didn't seem to notice how loud it was. She was just grateful that

Moxy was out there at all. And Aunt Susan Standish was snapping her fingers.

"It has a good beat, don't you think?" she said.

But no one could hear her.

chapter 83
In Which
Mrs. Maxwell Stops
Worrying About
Whether Moxy Will
Stop Playing "Heart
and Soul" When
It's Over

But before "Heart and Soul" was officially over, Moxy stopped playing.

chapter 84

In Which We Learn the Reason Moxy Stopped Playing "Heart and Soul" Before It Was Officially Over

Moxy stopped playing "Heart and Soul" before it was officially over for three very good reasons. They were:

1. The string around her neck that kept her cape on was strangling her.
2. She wanted to move on to the part of the show that she had rehearsed more—the bows.
3. She was suddenly very hungry.

chapter 85
BRAVA!

As soon as Moxy stopped playing, Pansy stopped playing. Then they walked to the center of the stage, holding hands. Then they held their hands up in the air the way heavyweight champions do and bowed and bowed—just the way they'd practiced a hundred times at home.

Here is a picture Mark took of Moxy and Pansy with their hands in the air.

Naturally, the applause went on and on
(or so it seemed to Moxy). And the longer
the applause went on, the longer the bows
went on. The bows went on for so long that

finally Moxy was forced to put her free hand in the air to settle the crowd down.

Here is a picture Mark took of Moxy's hand in the air. He called it "But Enough About Me."

"But Enough About Me," by Mark Maxwell.

chapter 86
Proceed with Caution—the End Is Near

After the recital came the after-recital party. It was a smashing success. Moxy could hardly catch her breath, there were so many people crowded around congratulating her—though no one asked for her autograph.

"The only thing missing," Moxy said in the car on the way home, "was a bouquet of roses to hold in my arms." Moxy was in the backseat with Mark and Pansy. They were counting to see how many cupcakes were left.

"Only seventy-five!" called out Pansy.

Moxy did some quick math. "That means," said Moxy, subtracting 75 from 150, "seventy-five people were watching me."

"Some people had more than one cupcake," said Mark.

"I had five," agreed Pansy.

"Still," said Moxy (who had eaten four cupcakes herself), "there were quite a few people out there. The applause was very loud."

"You didn't seem the least bit afraid," said Aunt Susan Standish. She turned around to look at Moxy.

"Oh," said Moxy, "*that*. I don't think I was ever really afraid. I think I was afraid of being afraid."

"Of course," said Aunt Susan Standish, turning back around. "And that's an entirely different thing."

Moxy was so excited about all the applause she'd gotten that she didn't know how she was going to fall asleep that night.

She wondered if sometimes you had to feel very bad in order to feel very good.

She rolled down the window and stuck her head out as far as she could without getting yelled at. The April air had that first-day-of-spring smell—a combination of old snow just melting and new mud just sprouting. The wind whipped her hair. She put her arm out and pretended it was a wing. It felt terrific to not feel afraid. Then she started to sing.

About the Author

Peggy Gifford is the author of *Moxy Maxwell Does Not Love* Stuart Little, which was chosen for Oprah's Book Club's Kids Reading List, and *Moxy Maxwell Does Not Love Writing Thank-you Notes,* praised by *Booklist* as "laugh-out-loud funny." Peggy holds an MFA from the Iowa Writers' Workshop and has worked as an editor for the Feminist Press and as an acquisitions editor for SUNY Press. She divides her time between New York City and South Carolina with her husband, Jack. You can visit Peggy and Moxy at www.peggygifford.com.

About the Illustrator

Valorie Fisher is the author and illustrator of several books, including *When Ruby Tried to Grow Candy*, *How High Can a Dinosaur Count?*, and *My Big Brother*. Her photographs for the Moxy Maxwell books have been called "fresh," "creative," "funny," and "snort-inducing." Valorie's photographs can be seen in the collections of major museums around the world, including the Brooklyn Museum, London's Victoria and Albert Museum, and the Bibliothèque Nationale in Paris. She lives in Cornwall, Connecticut, with her husband and their two children.